— Bats in the Schoolhouse Attic —

CARLA

THE CLUMSY BAT

 **Friesen**Press

Suite 300 - 990 Fort St
Victoria, BC, Canada, V8V 3K2
www.friesenpress.com

ISBN
978-1-4602-4747-1 (Paperback)
978-1-4602-4748-8 (eBook)

1. *Juvenile Fiction, Animals, Nocturnal*

Distributed to the trade by The Ingram Book Company

dedicated to
KAYLENE *and* **ROBYN**

Carla was beautiful and graceful soaring throughout the attic, flittering in and out of tiny holes. Her **EXQUISITE** wings were made of a thin, leathery skin stretching from her legs, over her arms and along her fingers. Carla shared a roost in the attic of the one hundred year old schoolhouse with thousands of others like herself.

Carla was a juvenile **YUMA BAT.**

Carla made a high pitched squeal when flying. The sound waves from Carla's squeal were invisible, and some were **ULTRASONIC.** People cannot hear ultrasonic sound waves.

The sound waves from Carla's squeal bounced off insects and other objects in her flight path. The sound waves then bounced back to her big ears as an **ECHO**. Carla's brain used the echo to make a **SOUND PICTURE** of the object in her mind. This is called **ECHOLOCATION.**

Using echolocation helped Carla find tasty insects to eat, and helped her fly extremely fast without bumping into things. Until one night when all of that changed: Carla the beautiful, Carla the graceful, mysteriously became a very **CLUMSY** bat.

On that mysterious night Carla was flying out of the schoolhouse dormer as usual when suddenly she was **KNOCKED** backwards against the wall! Had Carla really bumped into something? Or had she bumped into somebody? This never happened to her before! She had perfect echolocation.

Just then Grampy Bat stumbled past and said grumpily, "Carla, watch where you're flying. Don't be so **CLUMSY!**"

"Oh, I'm sorry Grampy Bat!" apologized Carla, holding the bump on her head. Grampy Bat had already flown off, so Carla continued on her way, too.

Carla didn't have much luck catching food on that mysterious night. Something wasn't right! But what was it?

CARLA WAS STUMPED.

Eventually, just before sunrise, Carla flew home to the attic with a grumbling tummy and a sore head. When Carla was home she bandaged her head, then curved her little claws into a timber beam, and fell asleep upside down, **GRUMPY** and **HUNGRY.**

When
Carla awoke the next night all the other bats teased her about bumping into Grampy Bat, and her **BANDAGED** head.

Carla felt awful. Instead of flying out of the roost with all the other bats, Carla waited patiently for everyone to leave. Once she was alone, Carla soared slowly towards the vent, and then flew cautiously, into the darkened sky. But as careful as she was, Carla **CLIPPED** one of her beautiful wings on the schoolhouse sign.

"Oh no," groaned Carla, "Not **ANOTHER** clumsy night!"

Throughout the night Carla flew around

the schoolyard desperately trying to catch insects. Carla scooped only a few bugs into her wings, and even that was difficult. Usually she was an excellent hunter, but **NOT** anymore; something wasn't right.

Suddenly Carla's echo created a picture of a massive bug in her brain! The **SCRUMPTIOUS** treat was right in front of her. Carla flew towards the target and opened her wings wide to draw the delicious morsel into her mouth.

"OUCH, OUCH, EEK!" squealed Carla.

What happened? She hurt all over! What had she captured? Carla slowly opened her wings expecting to see a humongous moth. There was no moth. There was only a prickly **PINECONE.**

What happened to Carla's echolocation? Why did the falling prickly pinecone show up as a picture of a humongous bug in her head?

WHAT WAS WRONG? WHY WAS SHE SO CLUMSY?

Carla, aching all over, slowly made her way back to the roost, in search of more Band-Aids.

Carla was getting **HUNGRIER** and **GRUMPIER** as each night passed. She didn't want to hurt herself anymore. And how could she catch dinner when her radar system clearly wasn't working?

Suddenly Carla had an idea!

"IT'S BRILLIANT!" squealed Carla as she rummaged through an old chest on the attic floor.

"Here it is," squealed Carla triumphantly, pulling a tiny **HEADLAMP** out of the chest and fitting it gently over her bandaged head.

"It fits perfectly!" squealed Carla excitedly as she turned on the headlamp switch, and flew off.

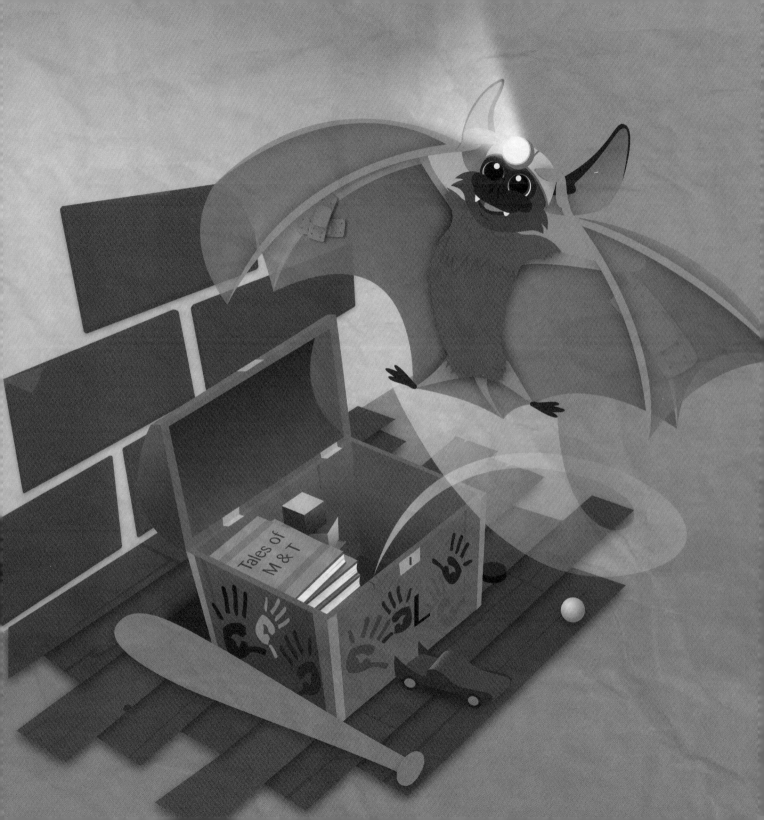

Throughout the
night Carla caught a feast of insects with her little
headlamp shining so brightly. She was feeling so
much better.

Then suddenly,

CLAMP!

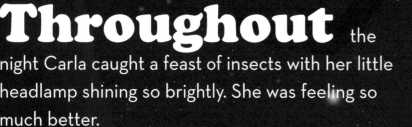

"OUCH! MY WING! WHAT IS THAT?"
squealed Carla in fright. When Carla tried to
squeal a second time, her squeal was gone.

SHE WAS FRANTIC!

Children in the park had been catching fireflies in
bug jars when they mistakenly captured Carla, with
her brightly shining headlamp! The lid of the jar
clamped **DOWN** tightly on Carla's delicate wing.

The children were surprised when they looked in their bug jar. They knew this little critter wasn't a firefly, but was it a bat? They had seen many bats before, but none of those bats had a bright **LIGHT** shining between their pointy ears. None of those bats had **BANDAGES** on their bodies. And none of those bats opened their mouths without making a piercing **SQUEAL!**

The children were confused and frightened. They ran away **SCREAMING**, dropping the bug jar as they fled the schoolyard.

As the jar dropped to the ground the lid flew open and Carla was **FREED!**

With a very sore wing and a broken headlamp, Carla flew to safety. Then she flew slowly back to the roost, bandaged her bent wing, and **HID** high in the rafters.

The next evening Mother Bat was shocked when she found Carla! "Carla, you have more bandages, and a **BENT WING!** What happened?" squealed Mother Bat with worry.

"Oh, Mother," rasped Carla, "I bumped into Grampy Bat and the school sign. I caught a falling pinecone for dinner. Then I was **CAPTURED** as a firefly and **LOST** my squeal!" Suddenly Mother Bat was very concerned about her perfect, beautiful Carla.

"I know about Grampy Bat, the school sign, and the pine cone. But what is this about a firefly and losing your squeal?" asked Mother Bat with alarm.

"Yes, my squeal is **GONE**," rasped Carla. **"AND I HURT ALL OVER."**

Mother Bat knew something was seriously wrong. She quickly flew off to find a thermometer to check Carla's **TEMPERATURE.**

"Well, NO WONDER!"** said Mother Bat with relief as she read the thermometer. "Carla, you have a very high temperature. Your soft squeal made only a **SMALL ECHO**; that means the sound waves weren't working. Then you lost your squeal completely! Your radar was broken. There was no picture! That's why you bumped into things and couldn't catch dinner. **YOUR ECHO WASN'T DOING IT'S JOB.** Carla, you have a virus, you're ill! Rest in the roost until you feel better," Mother Bat said gently.

Carla rested for three nights. As the moon rose on the fourth night, Carla yawned, shook off the bandages, stretched her beautiful wings, and tested her squeal.

"PERFECT!" she squealed with glee.

Carla soared throughout the roost, **EASILY** flittering through the dormer vent for her nightly feed. Carla the beautiful, Carla the graceful, Carla the perfect Yuma Bat had returned. Carla the Clumsy was **GONE FOREVER!**

BAT FACTS

Can bats really catch a cold or fever?

WHITE–NOSE SYNDROME is a virus currently spreading through North America, affecting hibernating bats.

A dusting of white powder appears across the nose and mouth of a bat affected by the virus.

White-nose Syndrome is **DESTROYING** many bat colonies; Scientists across the country are seeking a cure.

Using Echolocation

Bats call out **20** calls per **SECOND** when in **FLIGHT**.
Bats call out **200** calls per **SECOND** when **HUNTING**.

ABOUT THE AUTHOR

Darlene Hartford lives in Peachland, British Columbia with her husband. She enjoys an Okanagan lifestyle residing on Lake Okanagan, surrounded by nature. The series, Bats in the Schoolhouse Attic, includes her first published manuscripts, fulfilling a lifelong dream of writing children's books.

The lakefront community of Peachland has 5,000 residents, as well as a colony of 2,000 bats, that live in a historic schoolhouse. The school was closed and boarded shut for ten years. When the decision was made to preserve the building, the bat colony was also saved. A community educational program was established to promote public awareness of the value of bats, and to discredit myths surrounding the protected species. Darlene Hartford is the Peachland Chamber of Commerce Director of Peachland Bats Educational and Conservation Program.

The colony of winged mammals inspired Darlene Hartford to write a series of whimsical stories with endearing bat characters. The Peachland Historic Primary School is home to a maternity colony, consisting of mainly female bats, roosting together, producing offspring. The stories are adventures of mother bats with their pups or juveniles, and provide a harmonious balance between the imaginative and the educational. Each book provides Bat Facts in reference to the storyline.

Darlene Hartford dedicated the series, Bats in the Schoolhouse Attic, to her seven grandchildren.

CPSIA information can be obtained at www.ICGtesting.com
Printed in the USA
LVIW01n0854070315
429512LV00004B/10

* 9 7 8 1 4 6 0 2 4 7 4 7 1 *